Not for me, please!
I choose to act green

written by Maria Godsey
illustrated by Christoph J Kellner

D1303694

To my sons, Noah and Jonah, who have inspired this book
and my husband, Joseph, for his never-ending support

It can be difficult to understand the effect of our actions on the environment, especially when we don't see the damage or long term effects caused. We easily get trapped in our daily routine and habits without reflecting on the cost it has on our environment.

There once was a day when I didn't act green.
A time when I thought things would always stay clean.

I didn't think twice of the choices I made,
the impact they had, or the damage that stayed.

My actions were based on the ease brought to me,
with never much thought to our air, land, or sea.

However, with awareness of the effect of our behavior on our environment and planet, this can change. Understanding the interconnectedness and adjusting our way of living in a way that is friendly to our environment and sustainable for our planet means to think and act green.

But my thoughts around this
changed in a flash,
when I noticed the damage
caused by our trash.

Over 260 million tons of waste are generated every year in the United States. Globally, over 220 million tons of plastic are produced each year. All of this waste adds up and pollutes our environment, even if we don't see it all the time.

The sight of it caused a reaction in me,
and all I could say was "Not for me, please!"

Did you know that every piece of plastic ever created still exists today, with the exemption of plastic that has been incinerated? Our use of plastic has gotten so out of control that it is estimated there will be more plastic (by weight) in our oceans than fish by 2050.

I could not continue to live as I did;
surely I could help out, 'cause I'm a strong kid.

From there I decided that I will take action,
and protecting our planet became my new passion.

You, too, can help out with this phrase that I found.
Just say, "Not for me, please!" and stand your own ground.

It may take some practice, but I'll show you how, and why it's important for us to act now!

Each day, more than 500 million plastic straws are used and discarded in the United States alone. That's a lot of straws for just one country! This all creates waste that ends up in landfills and our oceans, just for the convenience of having a straw.

Let's look at a straw that comes with a shake.
Now imagine the trip this straw will soon take.

Most often our straws are made out of plastic
and after one use, they're thrown in a basket.

From the basket they head to the dump or the sea,
and become something known as marine debris.

Marine debris is human-created waste that has deliberately or accidentally been released in a lake, sea, ocean or waterway. In 2006, the United Nations Environment Programme estimated that there are 46,000 pieces of floating plastic in every square mile of ocean!

Our oceans are filled with all sorts of stuff,
that hurt our sea creatures and make their lives rough.

Poor turtles and fish mistake trash for their meal;
imagine the pain that their tummies must feel.

Or worse they get tangled in our careless muck;
around fins, heads, and legs, they're nothing but stuck!

Did you know about one truckload of trash is thrown into our waters every minute! This trash is captured by ocean currents and collects within ocean gyres or vortexes. Some gyres have become so full of trash that they have been nicknamed garbage patches. The Great Pacific Garbage Patch is now three times the size of France!

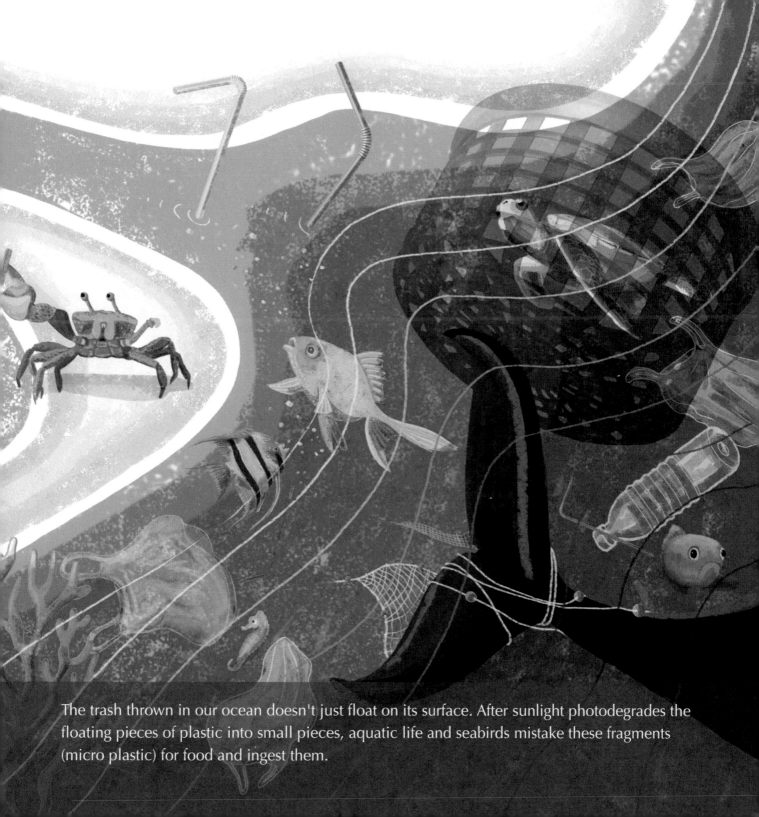

The trash thrown in our ocean doesn't just float on its surface. After sunlight photodegrades the floating pieces of plastic into small pieces, aquatic life and seabirds mistake these fragments (micro plastic) for food and ingest them.

Unfortunately, our sea life and birds are not the only ones ingesting plastic. When we eat fish that have eaten plastic, this too goes into our body. Additionally, plastic has frequently been found in many brands of bottled water.

This one little straw is not worth the high cost.
Why use things that harm or cause a great loss?

Here's where I'd say, "Not for me, please!" when asked.
I don't need a straw that will simply be trashed.

We all have a choice. Let's do our small part,
to refuse to cause harm and decide to act smart.

Did you know that 93 percent of Americans age six or older test positive for BPA (a plastic chemical)? Also, some of the compounds found in plastic have been found to alter hormones or have other potential human health effects.

Just think through your actions
and the cause and effect
of waste and pollution
and careless neglect.

Reduce, reuse and recycle (also known as the three R's) are the main ways to practice environmentally-responsible consumer behavior.

Let's choose to recycle,
reduce, and reuse;
and with my strong phrase,
there's no way we lose!

Here are some examples to
show what I mean,
and how you can join me and
begin to act green.

When we aim to reduce the amount of waste we produce, the consumption of new resources, reuse as many items as possible before replacing them, and recycle we take action to protect our environment and act green.

Do you see all this trash scattered around?
Why would anyone throw their stuff on the ground?

"Not for me, please!" is what I choose to say,
and pick up the litter to throw it away!

Recycling is the process of converting waste into new usable materials and objects. When we recycle, we reduce the need to consume Earth's natural resources through mining and forestry. Recycling helps ensure sustainable use of our limited resources.

I choose to be mindful and sort through my trash, recycling things like plastic or glass.

These can be turned into something brand new, like clothing, park benches, or even a shoe!

There are many things that can be recycled: metal, plastic, glass, aluminum, and paper. It's important to be concious that the items we buy are materials that can be recycled and not just end up in a landfill. Contact your local recycling center to find out what can be recycled in your area.

Look at these lights that someone left on,
in the room that is empty with everyone gone.

The same for computers, games and TVs,
why keep these things on for no one to see?

When you consume less power and energy, you decrease the demand and therefore emissions from power plants. To generate electricity, most power plants burn coal, crude oil or other fossil fuels. This method of creating energy is relatively inexpensive, but causes significant air pollution and contributes to climate change.

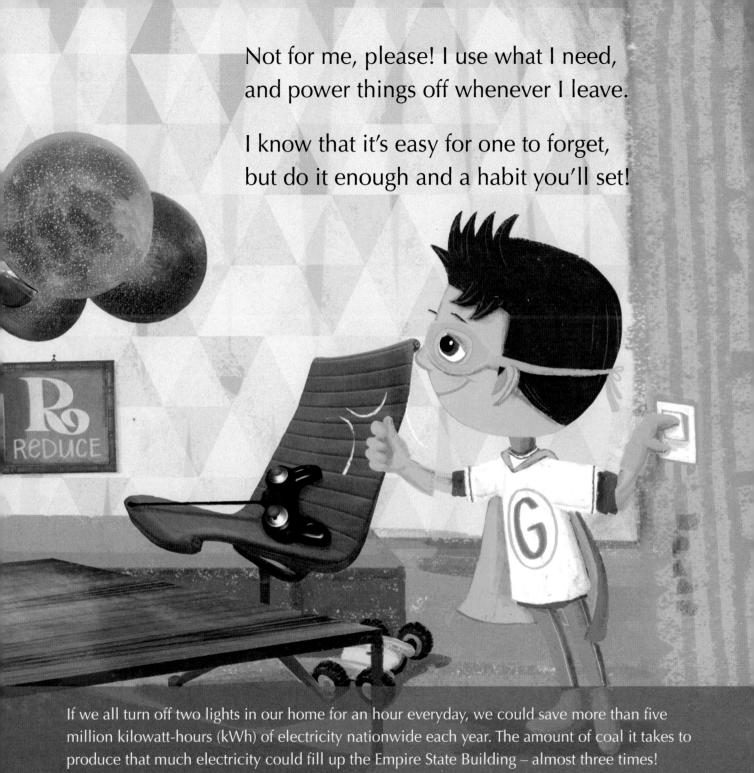

Not for me, please! I use what I need,
and power things off whenever I leave.

I know that it's easy for one to forget,
but do it enough and a habit you'll set!

If we all turn off two lights in our home for an hour everyday, we could save more than five million kilowatt-hours (kWh) of electricity nationwide each year. The amount of coal it takes to produce that much electricity could fill up the Empire State Building – almost three times!

Do you see this faucet and the water that flows?
How much has been wasted? It's so hard to know!

Just running the water when it's not in use,
is careless and wasteful; there's just no excuse!

According to Water.org, less than one percent of the water on the earth is readily available for human use. Salt can be removed from the sea water, but this process is expensive. Water conservation is a sustainable way to make the most of the fresh water that we do have.

Not for me, please! I avoid wasteful drips,
while brushing or cleaning my small fingertips!

We're lucky to have clean water to drink,
not the kind that is harmful, dirty or stinks!

Did you know a five-minute shower uses more water than a person in a developing country uses in a day? Sadly one in nine people worldwide do not have access to safe and clean drinking water. This lack of clean water kills children at a rate equivalent to a jet crashing every 4 hours.

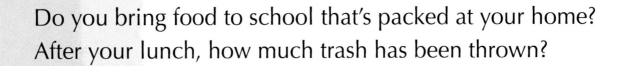

Do you bring food to school that's packed at your home?
After your lunch, how much trash has been thrown?

From plastic baggies to small boxes of juice,
it's scary the trash just one meal can produce!

It has been estimated that on average a school-age child, using a disposable lunch daily, generates 67 pounds of waste per school year. That equates to 18,760 pounds of lunch waste for just one average-size elementary school. Just by changing what and how you pack your lunch, can drastically reduce waste.

Not for me, please! I watch what I bring,
use food containers and avoid plastic things.

I bring my own bottle, I wash and reuse,
no need to contribute to plastic abuse!

On average, Americans use about 50 billion water bottles every year and only 23% of these
plastic water bottles are recycled. Just in the United States, 1.5 million barrels of oil are used
annually in the production of plastic bottles. If that oil was not used to make these bottles, it could
fuel 100,000 cars for a whole year.

Even while shopping, I see so much waste;
plastic grocery bags found all over the place!

And why are there so many things plastic wrapped?
Most of this plastic will only be scrapped!

Every year, Americans throw away over 140 billion food and drink containers and bottles. More than 30% of our waste is simply packaging material alone.

Not for me, please! I've had enough.
I use my cloth bags when I pack up my stuff.

I also take care of what goes in my cart.
Choosing less packaging and plastic is smart!

Plastic bags are created using fossil fuels and require vast amounts of water and energy to manufacture and ship. Plastic bags are used on average for twelve minutes, but remain in landfills, oceans, and other places for thousands of years.

Have you been on a picnic when the sky was bright blue?
Do you remember the cups, plates and forks that you used?

They were probably plastic and used only once,
but decomposing takes YEARS, not just a few months!

About 50 percent of plastic we use only once and throw it away. There are several kinds of plastic and each degrades at a different rate. The average time for a plastic bottle to completely degrade is at least 450 years. It can even take some bottles 1000 years to biodegrade!

Not for me, please! I'll join the ban
against single use plastic, 'cause I'm not a fan.

All that I need can come from my home;
let's avoid needless buys and reuse what we own!

Single-use plastics are plastic materials that are disposable and generally used only once before they are thrown away or recycled. Plastic water bottles and plastic bags are the most common single-use plastics. Did you know that France passed a law, which will go into effect in 2020, banning plastic plates, cups and utensils?

Our world is connected with resources shared.
We all must pitch in and give nature our care.

Let's pass on these things that don't make much sense,
or benefit us at our planet's expense.

The options are endless, if you make the right choice.
Think the three 'R's' and use your strong voice.

So how will you choose next time when you're out?
Will you think differently and take a new route?

You are free to borrow my little phrase,
and say, "Not for me, please!" in all of your days!

REFLECTIONS

Luke has shared many examples with us of how he chooses to act green. As well, he explained the impact our everyday choices make on our environment, sea life and animals. Luke has taught us about the three R's and how he applies these in his daily life. Let's reflect on these examples and what it means to act green. Here are some questions to help in this reflection.

What does it mean to you to think and act green? Do you think and act green?

Can you give some examples of how you think and act green at home or at school?

Do you remember the three R's? What does it mean to you to reduce, recycle or reuse? How can you do this in your everyday life?

How do you think you can better conserve water? Why do you think this is important?

What ways can you reduce the amount of energy you use? Why is it important to reduce our energy consumption?

Why is plastic harmful? What is the difference between single use and recyclable plastic?

Are there ways you can reduce your use of plastic (particularly single use plastic)? Could you even eliminate it from your everyday life?

How does it make you feel to learn of the harm being done to our planet and animals?

What do you think is preventing our society from acting green? What can be done about this? What role can you play?

How has Luke's story impacted you? Are there changes you would like to make at your school, at your home, or while your're just out and about?

Not for me, please!
ISBN-10: 1986909328
ISBN-13: 978-1986909327

Requests for additional information, working books, or permissions should be addressed to
info@lukes-choices.com

www.lukes-choices.com
@lukeschoices

Printed by CreateSpace, An Amazon.com Company
1.10

Made in the USA
Monee, IL
19 June 2020